This Little Tiger book belongs to:

_____

_____

_____

For Johnny and Ronnie,
and for Chloe, Oliver and Ben, for sharing - S. A. G.

LITTLE TIGER PRESS LTD,
an imprint of the Little Tiger Group
1 Coda Studios,
189 Munster Road, London SW6 6AW
www.littletiger.co.uk

First published in Great Britain 2013
This edition published 2019
Text and illustrations copyright © Sally Anne Garland 2013, 2019
Sally Anne Garland has asserted her right to be identified
as the author and illustrator of this work under the
Copyright, Designs and Patents Act, 1998
All rights reserved • ISBN 978-1-78881-464-5
LTP/2700/2546/1218
Printed in China
2 4 6 8 10 9 7 5 3 1

It's not always easy to...

Share

by Sally Anne Garland

LITTLE TIGER

LONDON

This morning I got up, ready to play—
Dad said, "Your **cousin**
is coming today.

He's only little, so
show him you care.

Please remember,
it's important to **share**."

As soon as
he came,
he wanted
my bear.

Dad said,
"Remember, please
let him share!"

He poked and **p u l l e d** him—

poor little Ted!

So I went to play...

... with my
dolls instead.

But he was behind me—
he followed me there!

Dad said, "He wants to play,
please let him **share**."

He jumped and bumped, and bounced on my bed.
I gave up doing that and...

... played dress-up instead.
He followed me,
wanting to see
what I'd wear.

Dad said, "He's having fun,
please let him **share**."

He grasped
and
grabbed—
my
beads fell

and

s p r e a d .

I gave up doing
that and...

. . . read my book instead.

He was there in a flash,
  as I chose Princess Clare.
Dad said, "He wants to see,
  please let him share."

He jostled and jiggled around as I read.

I gave up doing that and...

... watched TV instead.

He followed me in
and started to stare.

Dad said, "He likes it,
please let him
share."

He **bobbed** and **blocked** my view with his head.

I gave up doing that and...

... started painting instead.

He followed me again
and climbed on a chair.
Dad said, "He's copying,
please let him **share**."

He **scribbled**
and
scrawled—

"My picture!" I said.

I gave up doing that and...

... had lunch instead.
He ran into the kitchen and reached for my pear.
Dad said, "He's hungry, please let him **share**."

He grabbed at my plate

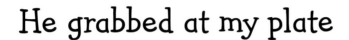

and it fell

to the floor.

I huffed
and
puffed,

and walked out the door!

All that he wants is to be
just like you.
That's why he copies
whatever you do!"

When my aunt arrived

she saw my despair.

"Just wait," she said,
        "Now it's *his* turn to share."

He hugged and squeezed me.

"Thank you," he said.

Then he was gone...

... and I sort of **missed** him instead.